D0574376

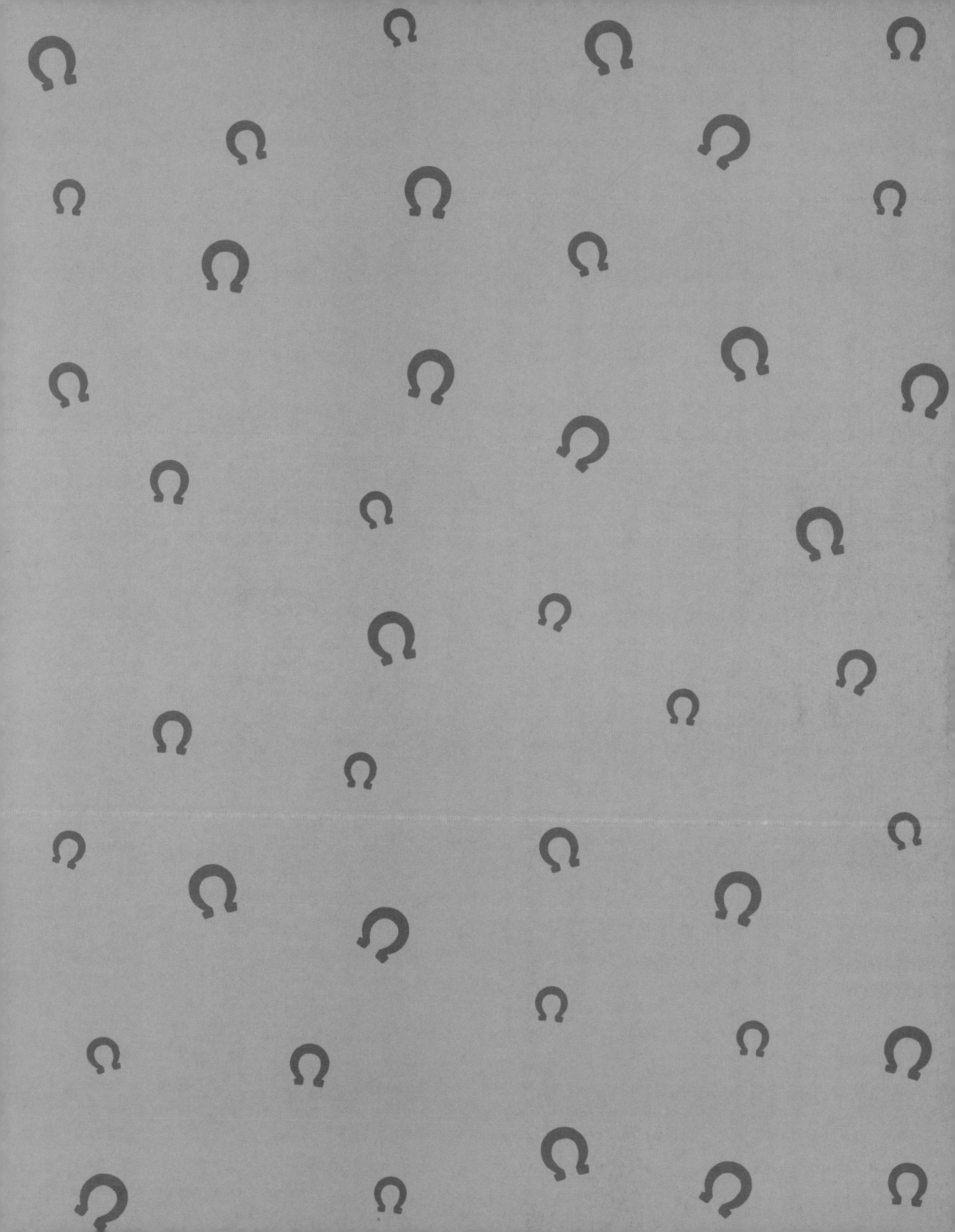

This edition published by Parragon Books Ltd in 2016

Parragon Books Ltd
Chartist House
15–17 Trim Street
Bath BA1 1HA, UK
www.parragon.com

Based on an episode by Laurie Israel and Rachel Ruderman
Adapted by Catherine Hapka
Illustrated by Grace Lee

ISBN 978-1-4748-2766-9

Printed in China

The Secret Library

Written by
Craig Gerber
and
Catherine Hapka

Illustrated by
Grace Lee

I'm Sofia.

Ever since I became a

princess,

my life has been full of adventure!

Today, Amber, James and I are having a race.

Just as we get started ...

… I see **Aunt Tilly!**

I love it when she comes to visit!

Back at the castle,
Tilly asks if I've read the
book she gave me. "I'm still
on chapter 12," I say.

"Wait till you get to chapter 17," she says.
"That's my favourite."

Up in my room, I turn to chapter 17 and find
a smaller book hidden in the pages.
It tells of secret passageways hidden
throughout Enchancia Castle!

Suddenly, my amulet glows blue. It leads me to
a wall, where I discover one of the passageways!

I follow my amulet's light through the opening and into a **maze** of passageways under the castle.

Finally, I come out beside an underground canal, where there's a boat waiting for me.

The boat takes me to a stairway
leading to a pair of locked doors.
Hmmmm. The **lock** is
shaped like my book!
Could the book be the key?
I try it - and it works!

"Wow! Where am I?"

A familiar voice answers:

"In the Secret Library."

It's Aunt Tilly! She says the library is filled with real-life stories that need endings.

"I'm the **storykeeper**," she says.
"It's my job to help finish the stories.
And now, I'm hoping that job will be yours."

"You want **me** to be the storykeeper?" I ask.
Aunt Tilly nods. "Here comes your first story now."

A magical book suddenly flies off the shelf. It's called

The Tale of Wildwing Valley.

It's the story of a flying horse named Mazzimo.
He lived in a royal stable but longed to be wild.
So he left in search of a place called Wildwing Valley,
where enchanted animals roam free.

But Mazzimo was captured by Prince Roderick and taken to the prince's castle in Borrea.

"That's awful!" I exclaim.

"It will be," Tilly says, "unless you give the story a better ending."

But I'm not sure I can do it on my own. So Aunt Tilly agrees to help me just this once.

We hurry to the stables.
When I tell Minimus about my mission,
he's surprised. Mazzimo is his
long-lost brother!

We fly to Borrea and soon find the royal stable.
It's huge, and everything is trimmed with gold.
"Mazzimo must be in there somewhere," I tell Aunt Tilly.
So we decide to split up and start searching the stable.

Minimus and I find Mazzimo in a locked stall.
"Good to see you, bro!" says Mazzimo.
"Can you get me out of here?"
Minimus looks around, confused. "But this is the nicest stable ever! Why would you want to leave?"

"Yeah, it's nice," Mazzimo says.
"But a cosy cage is still a cage.
I'd rather be free."
"Maybe we can talk about this
after we get out of here," I say.

Too late! Prince Roderick arrives with his stable master. The prince seems friendly at first – until I explain that we're here because Mazzimo wants to be free.

"You mean Thundercloud?" he says, pointing at Mazzimo. "He's my horse now."

"Can you believe he named me that?" Mazzimo mutters.

"Come on, Thundercloud," Prince Roderick says. "Let's go for a ride."

Then I get an idea.

When the prince opens the stall door, I yank on the rope he's holding to distract him.

"Fly for it, Mazzimo!" I yell.

Mazzimo bursts out of the stall and flies away!
Aunt Tilly and I jump on our horses and follow.

We did it! We **freed** Mazzimo!

But then we hear a shout behind us. It's **Prince Roderick** and his stable master chasing after us!

"Wildwing Valley is just ahead," Mazzimo says.

"Let's try to lose them in the gorges!" I shout.

We fly **super** fast, turning this way and that way through the twisty-turny ravines.

We lose the prince, but Minimus is upset with his brother. "Finding this valley is all you care about," he says. "When you took off, you didn't just leave the stable. You left Mum and Dad and me!"

Minimus is so upset he doesn't notice a tree up ahead. "**Look out!**" I cry.

He flies straight up
to miss the tree, but
I can't hold on!

"Gotcha!" Aunt
Tilly cries, catching me
just in time.

But her magical bag
gets knocked loose!

As we land, we look up to see that
Prince Roderick has caught up with us and
captured Minimus and Mazzimo!
We need Tilly's magical bag more than ever.
So we split up to find it.

I search high and low but with no luck. So far, I'm not a very good storykeeper. I lost Minimus AND Mazzimo. Maybe I'm not the right person for the job.

I notice my amulet glowing and then THUNK!

An arrow flies into a tree beside me!

I turn and gasp when I see

Princess Merida

step into view! My amulet

has brought her to help me.

When Merida hears my story, she smiles.
"All you need is the **belief** that you can
save them yourself. If you believe in yourself
and what you can do, your aim
will always be true."

Could Princess Merida be right? Maybe I **can** do it!

As I run back through the forest,
I spot Aunt Tilly's horse, so I jump on and take off.
Soon we catch up with Minimus and
Mazzimo, who are tied to Prince Roderick's horse.
Just as I jump on to Minimus and untie him,
Prince Roderick sees me.

All I have is Tilly's umbrella ...
and an idea. I swoop around,
hook the prince's belt with
the **umbrella**, and yank
him off his horse!

Then I send Aunt Tilly's horse
back for her and untie Mazzimo.
At last, **he is free!**

Mazzimo leads the way to the land
of his dreams - Wildwing Valley.

It's so **beautiful!**

Minimus turns to his brother.
"After being captured by Prince Roderick, I finally understand
how you felt when you were locked up in a stable."

"We may be different," says Mazzimo,
"but you're my brother, and I love you."
Minimus smiles. "I love you, too."

When we return to the Secret Library,
Aunt Tilly congratulates me for finishing my first story.
"So what's next?" I ask.
Aunt Tilly smiles. "Have a seat and find out ...

storykeeper!"

The End

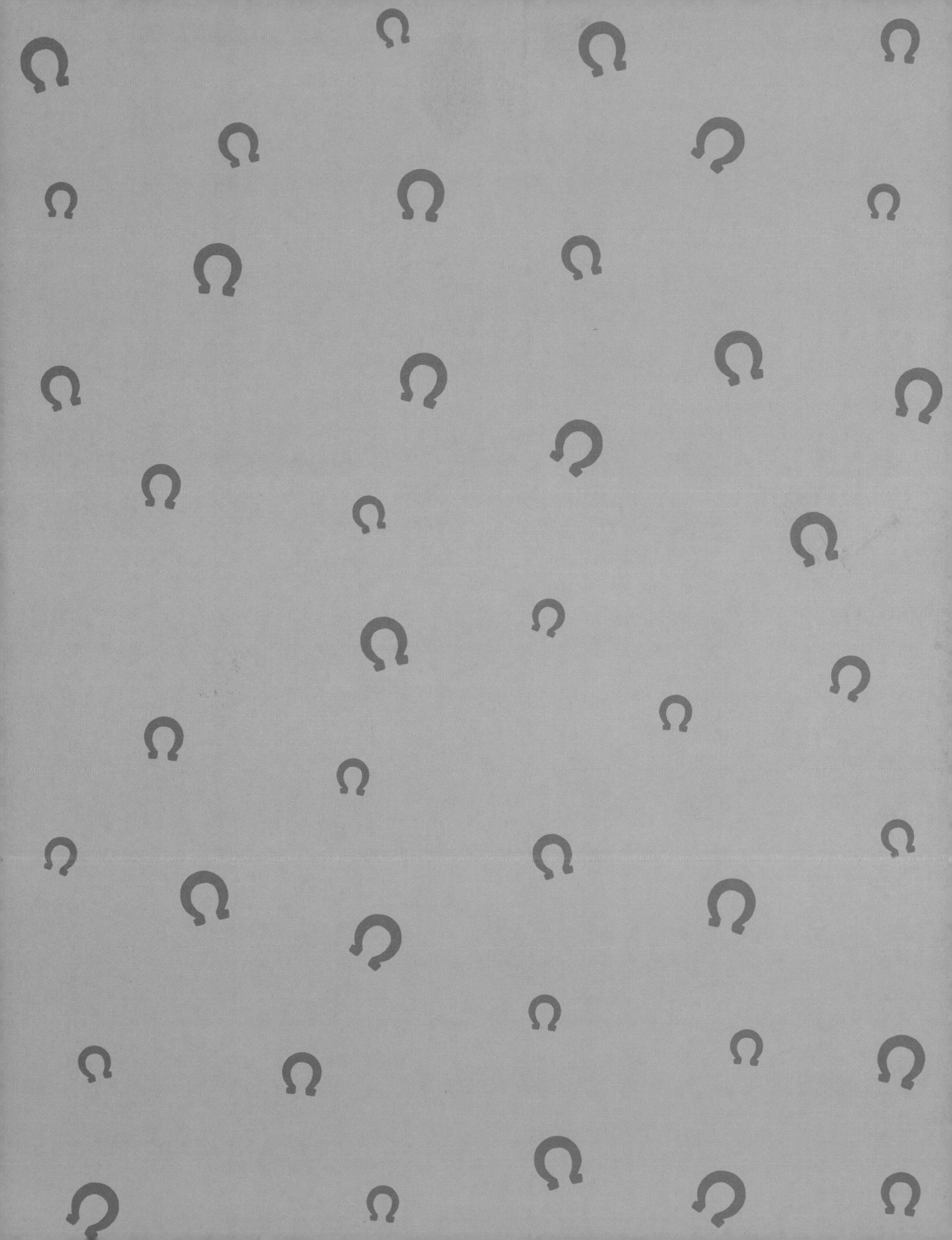